SURPRISE!

CAROLINE HADILAKSONO

SCHOLASTIC INC.

Bear, Raccoon, and Squirrel had been friends for a really long time.

"I'm bored," said Squirrel.

"I wish there was something more exciting to do," said Raccoon.

"I wish we had new friends to play with," said Bear.

But making new friends . . .

. . . isn't always easy.

They waited a long time for the right friend
to wander into their neck of the woods.

One day, their wait was finally over.

They'd heard of city folks, but they'd never seen any, until now.

Eagerly, they hatched a plot to convince the city folks to stay. "We need to do something splendid," said Bear.

"How about a Welcome Party?" said Raccoon.
"Yes, a surprise Welcome Party," said Squirrel.

"We will have the most splendid foods," said Raccoon.

"And the most splendid entertainment," said Squirrel.

"And the most splendid decorations," said Bear.

They were almost ready.

"Hmm, something is missing. I will be right back," said Bear.

It wasn't long until Raccoon and Squirrel heard footsteps. But it wasn't Bear who returned.

Finally, Bear returned . . .
with party hats for everyone!

GRAWW

But the guests were in a hurry to leave.

GGRAWW

BEAR!

GROARRRRR
RRAWRRR

"Don't leave! We have the most splendid food!" said Raccoon.

"We have the most splendid entertainment!" said Squirrel.

"You forgot your party hats!" said Bear.

They didn't know why the city folks left so soon.
But Bear, Squirrel, and Raccoon had a splendid time
together, just the three of them.

For the lonely reader

ISBN 978-1-338-32833-2

Arthur A. Levine Books hardcover edition published by Arthur A. Levine Books,
an imprint of Scholastic Inc., October 2018

The publisher does not have any control over and does not assume any
responsibility for author or third-party websites or their content.

12 11 10 9 8 7 6 5 4 3 2 1   19 20 21 22 23 24

Printed in the U.S.A.   40

This edition first printing, January 2019

The images in this book are a mix of watercolor paintings
and gouache textures, all combined and finished off digitally.
Book design by Christine Kettner